LITTLE MISS TROUBLE

and the Mermaid

Roger Hargreaves

Original concept by
Roger Hargreaves

Written and illustrated by
Adam Hargreaves

The trouble with Little Miss Trouble is that she is always causing trouble.

Like when she met Mr Greedy.

"Do you know that they are giving away ice-creams around the corner?" she asked him.

"Really!" cried Mr Greedy, and raced off to get some.

What he did not know, and Little Miss Trouble did, was that workmen had dug up the pavement around the corner.

Mr Greedy fell right down the hole. THUMP!

Little Miss Trouble thought this was very funny.

Mr Greedy did not.

Now, the trouble with making trouble is that sometimes it can catch up with you.

And that is what happened when Little Miss Trouble went to Seatown last week.

Her first two days in Seatown were great fun. Great fun for her, but no fun for anybody else!

She splashed Little Miss Splendid, and blamed Little Miss Chatterbox.

Who Little Miss Splendid sprayed with cold seawater!

Little Miss Trouble kicked sand all over Mr Strong and then blamed Mr Sneeze.

Who Mr Strong buried in sand up to his nose!

Little Miss Trouble was having the time of her life. She had never caused so much trouble!

On her third day in Seatown, she decided to go fishing with Mr Muddle and Little Miss Bossy.
The three of them rowed out to sea and set up their fishing rods.

Little Miss Trouble was trying to think of the best way to cause trouble when she felt something tug on her fishing line.

"I've caught a fish!" she cried, excitedly.

Then there was another tug. A much stronger tug. A tug so strong that it pulled her right out of the boat!

Not only did it pull her out of the boat, it pulled her down into the sea.

Little Miss Trouble let go of the fishing line, but something, or someone, grabbed her foot and dragged her deeper and deeper.

It was not until she reached the bottom of the sea
that she discovered who had caught her.

It was a mermaid!

"There is someone who wishes to see you," said
the Mermaid to a flabbergasted Little Miss Trouble.

"Take me back!" demanded Little Miss Trouble.

"Later," said the Mermaid. "Now, follow me."

Little Miss Trouble realised that she had no choice in the matter, so she did as she was told.

The Mermaid took Little Miss Trouble's hand and led her across the seabed.

After a short while, they came to a coral reef.

"Where are you taking me?" asked Little
Miss Trouble.

"You are about to find out," replied the Mermaid.

In the middle of the reef was a circle of sand and in the middle of the circle was a coral throne.

And sitting on the throne was the Mermaid Queen.

"I have brought Little Miss Trouble as you ordered, Your Highness," said the Mermaid.

"So you are the person who has been causing so much trouble on my beach and in my sea!" said the Mermaid Queen, angrily. "It is time that you learnt to behave yourself. No more splashing people and kicking sand around."

"But it wasn't me!" exclaimed Little Miss Trouble. "It was Little Miss Chatterbox and Mr . . . "

To Little Miss Trouble's huge surprise, the word 'sneeze', which she had meant to say, came out as a bubble. And every time she tried to say it, the same thing happened, until there was a stream of bubbles coming out of her mouth!

"It is no good you blaming other people and getting them into trouble," said the Mermaid Queen. "From now on, every time you try to make trouble, all that you will get for your trouble is bubbles! You may go back to the beach now."

The Mermaid led Little Miss Trouble away. They swam to the edge of the coral reef, where a dolphin was waiting.

"This dolphin will take you back to Seatown. Do not forget what the Queen said," warned the Mermaid.

Little Miss Trouble held on to the dolphin's fin and rode her back to the beach, where the dolphin left her at the shore.

The beach was crowded and as Little Miss Trouble watched the dolphin's fin as it swam away, an idea struck her.

"There's a . . . !" she shouted, at the top of her voice, but instead of the word 'shark', which she had meant to shout to scare everyone, a huge bubble came out of her mouth.

And then another.

Everyone on the beach gave her a very odd look.

Feeling very foolish, Little Miss Trouble went back to her hotel.

The next morning, she felt much better.

Down on the beach, she found Little Miss Sunshine sunbathing on a beach towel. Little Miss Trouble crept up behind her and dropped her ice-cream on to Little Miss Sunshine!

"What was that?" screamed Little Miss Sunshine, leaping up in surprise. "Who did that?"

"It was . . ." began Little Miss Trouble.

She was about to say, 'Mr Rush', but I am sure you know what came out instead.

That's right!

An enormous bubble!

And then more and more and more bubbles.

And that was not all.

"How could you!" cried Little Miss Sunshine,
and she threw what was left of the ice-cream at
Little Miss Trouble.

There was nothing Little Miss Trouble could say.

Because she could not speak.

All she could do was blow bubbles.

And so it went on.

Every time Little Miss Trouble tried to cause trouble, the same thing happened.

By the end of the week, Little Miss Trouble had given up trying to make trouble and had started building sandcastles instead.

In fact, she became so good at building sandcastles that she won the sandcastle competition! She was very excited, until she discovered what the prize was.

A year's supply of bubble bath!